THE SEVENTEEN EXECUTIONS OF SIGNORE DON VASHTA

**SIXTEEN EXECUTIONS HAVE FAILED.
THE SEVENTEENTH IS ABOUT TO BEGIN.**

Beal devoted his life to the study of executions.
The notorious Don Vashta is the greatest challenge any
executioner can face: an immortal criminal who always
rises from the dead to sin again.

A short story about a job that turns into a friendship,
and a friendship that becomes an obsession.

THE SEVENTEEN EXECUTIONS OF SIGNORE DON VASHTA

a BRAIN JAR PRESS short story chapbook

PETER M. BALL

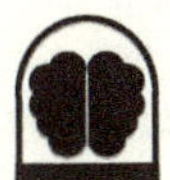

THE SEVENTEEN EXECUTIONS OF SIGNORE DON VASHTA

1.

Of the sixteen recorded executions featuring Signore Don Vashta as the subject, I have been present for three, and I have read detailed and verified accounts of another two.

In addition, I am known as a man who has an interest in such things, and thus I am a man to whom all rumors eventually find their way. Among our fraternity, if we can truly be called such, this makes me something of an expert, and I do not take this duty lightly.

As many of you know, I inherited this particular interest from one Roland K., who lived in the Americas and served as my mentor. It is with respect to the fidelity and accuracy of Roland's service that I leave this note to explain my most recent actions.

2.

Roland K. once sent a letter from his station in the Americas. In it, he detailed the events that led to his resignation and the dismissal from our ledgers that followed not long after.

"*It is a terrible thing to hang a man,*" his letter said, "*and I find I have no longer have the stomach for it, particularly in the manner that is utilized in these parts. There is no art to death here, no science as precise as the hangman's drop. There are no scaffolds to serve as the staging for the death, nor even the grotesque parody offered by a rope looped over a convenient branch. Instead, they affix the noose to the top of a great pole and raise the subject to it, hoisting him into position using a sling affixed beneath the arms.*

"*The subjects own weight is enough to begin the process, although it is slower than we have come to prefer. When the locals wish to hasten the subject's death, they place a second noose over the feet and several strong men pull down, speeding the asphyxiation that inevitably results in death. This is, despite the barbarism involved, the more humane method of execution given the limitations of their method.*

"*They did no such thing when Signore Vashta came to the noose.*

"*It's not the act that disables me so, but the anticipation of it. There is so much waiting, Beal, so much pageantry. Signore Vashta's crimes were minor, and he stood, resolute, while the theater of death played out. It's a terrible thing we do, Beal, a terrible, terrible thing. Those minutes he stood on the platform, adorned with noose and a black sack to obscure his features. Minutes spent listening, waiting, while they placed the sling around him.*

"*It is the sound of it that haunts me, my friend. The gurgle and croak of a man left to die. It is a terrible thing to be haunted, in our work.*

"*For days after the execution, I believed I saw the dead man dallying about town, seated in cafes or breaking his fast at the local hotel. I told myself that it cannot be, that the dead, of necessity, stay dead, and yet Signore Don Vashta's shade persists, an ever-present reminder of the things I have witnessed.*

"I fear I can no longer perform my duties. My reason becomes suspect, and our work must remain above reproach if we are to be trusted."

It is a matter of public record that Roland K. tendered his resignation two weeks after the mailing of this letter, and there are many who impugn his reputation when they speculate on his reasons for doing so.

I share these details with you today because his letter brings to light many things that I, too, have noticed in my years following Signore Vashta and his many executions.

It is true, as Roland K. notes, that it is not natural to kill a man, even one who cannot die such as Signore Don Vashta. It is true, as he notes, that a measure of pageantry is necessary. The pageantry creates the distance one needs to go through with the act, serves as the barrier between the executioner and despair.

We are protected by reason and the understanding of our role, both of which are threatened when Don Vashta returns from the grave.

3.

My own meeting with Signore Vashta took place here in the antipodes, when he was first incarcerated in the dismal Melbourne Jail, awaiting his inevitable demise at the hands of Her Majesty's firing squad.

It was, at the time, two days before his scheduled execution.

I should note that the firing squad was not the preferred method of execution in Melbourne at the time —any study of our records will show the locals shared a predilection for the noose—but even then the local correctional knew of Don Vashta's abilities.

And so an expert was called for, and so it became my duty to advise them on the correct procedures for elimination.

Don Vashta knew my role immediately, from the moment I entered his cell, and he rose from the Spartan cot to greet me like an old friend, kissing me upon each cheek before clasping me to his chest. "Sir," he said, whispering so that I alone could hear him, "whatever you do tomorrow, do your duty. I must demand that you kill me, for I fear I am a villain and cannot be trusted to continue walking this earth."

I told him, as we all do, that it is not our place to punish the accused. We act from a place of reason, doing as duty demands. We leave it to others to apportion blame and decide the guilty's punishment.

Don Vashta seemed to grasp this and released me from his grip. "Do not fear, sir," he said. "I welcome any man who can finally end my time here on earth. When your men shoot—"he thumped his chest with a fist "—aim here, aim true, I beg you."

It was, I learned, to be his fourth execution, although only the second to use the firing squad as their means of disposal. He'd last faced such a punishment in the early days of the First World War, and it had proved no more effective than the morning he was hung.

I asked him, years later, why he expected my squad to succeed where others had already failed.

"Ah, Beal," he said, and lifted an ice-cooled drink to his lips. "I no longer desired to live, my friend, by the time the two of us met. I believed that would make the difference, and in that I was twice a fool."

4.

I will note, here, that Signore Bashta is prettier than one might expect after hearing of his legend. His eyelashes are long and delicate as a woman's, and his lips are thin and exquisite in their cruelty. We shall not speak of his blade-like cheeks, nor the endless sorrow in his eyes. Only the loss of his left ear mars the symmetry of his features, and even that is normally covered by the habit of growing his hair long.

On the night before his seventh execution, he asked me for a woman. We were in the Americas, and my presence in his cell was purely a courtesy. I had no power here, far from home, beyond my familiarity with the subject and my reputation as an expert in his condition. They wanted me present to advise them and ensure the execution took. My response was that there could be no such guarantee, but they flew me over anyway and put me up in a cheap motel a few minutes away from the prison.

"If it's to be my last night," Don Vashta said, "I would rather like a woman to see me off to whatever comes next. I don't suppose you could organize that, Beal?"

"That is not in my power," I told him, and he sighed and nodded.

"I would go myself," he said, "but, well, you know." He waved his hands at the bars, at the concrete walls and the prison guards, the cameras that watched his ever movement.

"I never had problems getting women, Beal," he said. "Perhaps that is part of my curse, eh?"

"You are a handsome man, Signore."

"I am," he agreed, "but I'll not be so pretty tomorrow."

He sniffed and lay his head against the thin pillows of his cot. "Pity."

I could not tell you what moved me, this time and this time alone, but I made him an offer: "I could ask them to try poison instead. It will be considerably less messy."

Signore Vashta shook his head. "For a man of my proclivities," he said, "not being pretty is one of the few punishments the law can afford. There will be other women eventually, Beal, unless we finally get this right."

He smiled at me, and winked, then rolled over to go to sleep. I waited there through the evening, in case he had more to say.

The next morning they took him to the chamber. I sat in a small, concrete room with a governor and a lawyer and a weeping woman I could not recognize. At 10:15 the lights in the room flickered, and for the space of several minutes afterwards we let ourselves believe that this time, yes, this time, Don Vashta was truly dead.

5.

Signore Vashta lost his right ear during his third execution. It was torn off by a noose that was incorrectly applied, and this alone, of all his maladies, remains uncured and unhealed in the aftermath. I have long believed that solving the riddle of this scar, understanding why it alone remains with him, lies at the heart of resolving the problem Don Vashta represents.

Alas, I no longer have theories on how this scarring achieved. It is, like many things, a mystery beyond my understanding.

6.

By the eve of his thirteenth execution, it had become known amongst our fraternity that I was a man with an interest. There would be letters, sometimes as many as three in a week, from those who claimed to be present at Signore Don Vashta's final death. Many of these proved to be false, a charlatan's attempting to impress me with their made-up tales, or misguided efforts by junior members with too much faith in their skills.

One letter, in all those years, bore the ring of truth.

"My dear Beal," it began, *"I am writing to inform you of the most extraordinary incidents that accompanied the execution of a rogue known as Don Vashta, which I have been led to believe, by the friend of a friend, may be of some considerable interest to you.*

"I understand that you are familiar with the man I speak of—a rake and villain of considerable charm—and have previously served as an advisor for those in my position. He has been accused of great crimes in my country, and such crimes are punishable by beheading when the perpetrator is caught. Though it took us many moths, we acquired Signore Vashta while he broke his fast in a small cantina on the coast.

"It is my understanding that he came quite peacefully, despite having eaten only one of the three hard-boiled eggs he had ordered.

"We knew of him by reputation, although reputations are lacking in details, as I'm sure you are aware. It wasn't until I saw the scars on Signore Vashta's body, fading despite the application of a lash just three days before, that I truly believed such a man could exist. I did not believe in immortality, and still I do not, but perhaps some mark of the devil accompanies the criminal Vashta and saves him when others will perish.

"It was a humid morning when it came time to do my duty. Ordinarily we would have favored the gallows, but we knew

there was no joy in attempting such a death. The task of finding a death that would finally bring Signore Vashta peace fell to me.

"I feel a great shame in my final decision, although I spoke with Don Vashta before implementing it. We fed him great quantities of acid, of the hydrochloric kind, a method I borrowed from a particularly lurid novella I read in my childhood years. It was horrible to do, worse to experience, but in the final moments I believed I'd succeeded where other's failed. Don Vashta had been executed, although it was a cruel and debased death.

"I could not have done this to him, had he not asked me to do so. He wanted to die, badly, and no longer believed you would help him do so.

"We interred him in a traitor's grave. For days we believed he remained there, dead as any other victim of the executioner's art.

"Before the week was out we heard rumors of his presence in the countryside, feasting at the same cantina where we'd acquired him a week earlier. Upon hearing this, I went to see him. He spoke with a cold rasp, so it seems my cruelty had left some faint mark upon him and I had not the heart to report his presence to my superiors.

"I may be a patriot, Mister Beal, but I am not cruel. No matter what Don Vashta has done, I do not wish him to experience such pain again.

"I told him I would not arrest him again, although I begged him to leave the country. Eventually he agreed, and suggested I contact you to explain my actions.

"I do so now, although it shames me to make this admission. You have my respect, sir, for sticking with Don Vashta's case for so long as you have, particularly in light of the inevitable hopelessness of your cause.

"Yours, F."

I did not respond to Monsignor F.'s letter. There was

little I could offer him that would make sense of what he'd
seen.

7.

I have no record of Don Vashta's fourteenth execution,
but I still hope to hear of the method used. It is one of
three gaps in my otherwise comprehensive file.

8.

His fifteenth execution saw him drawn and quartered by a
quartet of wild brumbies. An impromptu response to an
insult he offered a local while the two us traveled through
South America. I can still remember the look of glee on
his face as they took him out and secured the chains on his
wrists and ankles.

"Don't you understand, Beal? After all this time? At
last, we have some novelty."

He grinned as they fired their rifles and the horses star-
tled, bolting in all four directions. Signore Vashta was not
a big man. It didn't take long for the horses to do their job.

It was here, we discovered, that dismemberment
served as an inefficient means of disposing of the subject.
He returned, whole and fully healed, several days after his
death, joining me in my carriage as our train traveled over
the mountains.

I dissembled and queried how this might have
happened.

"I do not wish to speak of it," Signore Vashta said,
although he showed me the scars where his limbs had been
rejoined. They were healing, albeit slowly. Today they are

but white marks against the Don Vashta's tanned skin, and one day even those will fade and leave him unblemished.

9.

There are those, upon finding that I traveled with the man, who find my interest in his executions unsavory.

I make no apologies for my friendships.

10.

The most extraordinary aspect of Don Vashta's situation lies the reaction he provokes. He claims to be an evil man, and there are no shortage of crimes attributed to his name, but in truth he is no more evil than many who have suffered the wrath of the law and significantly less evil than most.

Don Vashta is a seductive man, charming in his own way. This is coupled with a streak of cruelty and a thorough disregard for convention, which often sees him accused of an abundance of crimes when others would face a singled charge. That one likes the man, yet loathes themselves for it, is, perhaps, at the heart of the response he evokes from judiciary officials.

11.

When the Government Man first came to my house, I asked him a single question. "What is the method of execution?"

The Government Man is short and officious, with a mean haircut and a sallow face. He wears salmon colored shirts that do not suit his complexion. He fidgets and pulls out a handkerchief, coughing into it politely when he realizes there's no other reason to have pulled it from his pocket.

"Well," he said, "he's been charged—"

"Not the charges, just the punishment."

I have no use for charges. Now, after all this time, what is one more charge laid at Don Vashta's feet?

"Oh," the Government Man said, and he fidgeted some more. "Well, we wanted your help with that, but we were thinking, maybe...poison?" He peeks at me, furtively, trying to gauge my reaction.

I gave him nothing. "What kind?"

"The...usual kind?"

"Ah," I said, "potassium chloride and all the trimmings. I wish you luck, sir, for his sake and yours."

The Government Man, more astute than many in his position, raised an eyebrow. "You do not think this will work, sir?"

I assured him I did not. "Signore Vashta has been poisoned before," I said, "with substances far worse than the ones you propose."

When he asked me for options, I ventured, perhaps, a wood-chipper would be in order. Perhaps we should simply fire Don Vashta into space and let the vacuum do its grisly work.

The Government Man looked at me, as if I might be joking.

If I am honest, dear colleagues, I could not tell you whether I was or was not.

12.

I asked him, once, what the secret was. How he, of all people, returned after every death. We were in a cantina down on the coast. It had been twenty years since they'd executed him here, and Don Vashta had been overcome with a feeling of nostalgia. When I asked the question he ceased eating his eggs, placed his knife and fork on the table and stared out over the gentle sea.

"At first I thought it was me," he said. "I didn't want to die, so somehow, I simply didn't. Willpower, you know? Or, perhaps, some strange blessing.

"Then the bad days came and I wanted to be punished, but no-one could ever achieve it for longer than a few days. I tried many things and I was planted in the ground, and yet I would return three days later like clockwork, walking into town with no real memory of where I'd been. Those were the worst, Beal. Those years turned me into a monster, and I indulged every whim. A man who cannot die is a man who doesn't fear, and a man who doesn't fear-
-"

He shrugged and drank his coffee, returned to his eggs.

"These days the deaths are just something that happens. I try not to think about it, and take my pleasures where they come, accepting that one day the inevitable will happen if I but wait my turn."

"Accept?" I said.

"It is better than hope," Don Vashta said. "A man can accept many things, but hope is a knife that digs in his heart until it drives him mad."

13.

Just a few minutes ago, I received the phone call. They are moving Don Vashta by van, transporting him to the site of his seventeenth execution, and they wish me to come along and observe his latest death. A man from the government has been pestering me for days, despite the fact I tell him that I have no interest in such things anymore.

"But you must," the man says, time and again, "He's asked you to be there."

"And I owe Don Vashta nothing, so he has no power to compel my attendance."

"Your government is requesting your presence, sir."

"They," I tell him, "have even less power to compel me than Signore Don Vashta does."

The Government Man says nothing to this. Perhaps he cannot comprehend it, being free of the government's influence. They have sent him to my house three times in preparation for this day, trying to convince me to do my duty.

"Sir," the Government man says, "I must re-assert that-
-"

I do not let him finish. "I am not coming, sir," I tell him. "My government can go to hell."

14.

There are those who believe Don Vashta is the devil, and those who believe he is nothing but a hoax, and yet others who are convinced that he has achieved some scientific breakthrough that should be shared with the world.

I have known Don Vashta for many years, have seen

him killed thrice and advised on many other deaths, and none of these theories ring true. I can offer you no better explanations, not venture any theories. I was done with such things years ago, and do not wish to return to the habits of a younger self. I do not care to know the mysteries of the world, lest they cease to be mysteries and become drab and plain.

In this, perhaps, I share something with Roland K., who saw a man hung and turned away. I feel, perhaps, a kinship with him, that I haven't felt in a considerably long time.

15.

It should be noted, even today, that Don Vashta remains handsome and young. The stories he can tell you about his various incarcerations, the times he has been locked away or captured by those who experiment on him. He has suffered many forms of punishment and endured them all, knows tricks of escaping prisons and labs that no other man could know.

Don Vashta has a knack for storytelling that I, for my sins, find lacking. Often these stories are brilliantly fantastic and loaded with salacious detail.

This document concerns itself only with Signore Don Vashta's executions, as befits the records of a man with my interests and experiences.

16.

I am old and I am cantankerous and I fear that my reason is slipping. In truth, I would be at the execution today, but I fear I can no longer perform as needed. My duty to our fraternity has long given way to my duty towards my friend, seeking a means of achieving that which he most desires.

And I fear I bring us into disrepute, despite my best efforts to remain above approach.

The man from the government called me again, asking for clarification on the methods I have suggested. They're going to try them, one after the other, in an effort to rid the earth of the scourge known only as Signore Don Vashta.

He repeated the request that I witness Don Vashta's death, and once again I declined.

17.

It is late. A man from the government waits, in a car, outside my home. He knocked on my door when he first arrived, introduced himself and offered to drive me to the prison. "I know you've said you aren't interested, sir," he told me, "but they wanted me here in case you changed your mind."

I offered him a cup of tea, which he refused. Then he went back to his car and settled into the front seat, reading a magazine by the dim interior light.

The hours advance, merciless as an invading army. I await the phone call that, inevitably, will come, informing me of the exact time and method of Don Vashta's execution, the various indicators they choose to believe are proof their endeavor has been a success.

I will write details down, for that is the nature of duty. If you are one who has taken an interest, then you live up to the obligations that come with that role. It matters not if you have befriended the man, overlooked his terrible nature and the evil in his past. Duty, it must be said, is duty.

Although even this has limits.

I no longer know which phone call bothers me more, the inevitable call informing me of his death, or the one that will come later, days after the authorities lose interest in my actions, when a familiar voice will greet me like a co-conspirator and offer a new report.

He will tell me the things he recalls of this death, and the things he recalls of his journey back. There is no joy in this, no mercy in his recollection. It would be easier if I did not answer, but this, too, is duty. And I know that the wait is the worst of it.

It is a long wait, a terrible wait.

At least, for me, there is the knowledge that an end will come.

How unbearable must it be to wake and wake again, to know that one's death is forever out of reach?

18.

Thrice now, in our conversations, he has made me an offer to travel together as we once did. "Beal, old friend," he says to me, "I could use a companion, and there is but one man I trust."

It may be a lie, for I know he's a liar, but thrice now I've elected to deny his offer and remain faithful to my appointed task. Even now, as my fidelity to duty wanes, a part of me longs to keep to the path.

I write this now, from my station here in the antipodes, and I no longer have the strength to decline his offer if he asks again.

After this, his seventeenth execution, I will acquiesce

to Don Vashta's request. I will tender my resignation and be struck from the ledgers, to step away from the pageantry and reason that protects us.

I do this willingly, with full knowledge of what it entails, and know there will be those who cast aspersions on my work once I stray, attempting to refute all I have done in the years before. I accept this also, and choose to go forth regardless.

I will not ask your forgiveness, for I know there can be no such. All I offer is an explanation, and even that a simple one: We forgive a great deal—perhaps too much—of those we already love. And if he asks, I will embrace my friend and pledge myself to travel beside him, watching over his future executions until such time I breath my last.

I do this not to learn his secret, but because all men deserve such, a friend to share their journey and ease the burden of troubles.

If this makes me a monster in the eyes of our fraternity, then I willingly accept the charge.

AUTHORS NOTE

I started writing this story in a friend's spare room back in 2012. The finished version appeared in Daily Science Fiction two years later, introducing the world to the unlikely friendship between Don Vashta and the execution, Beal.

No story emerges from a vacuum, and this one developed around a divergent set of influences and inspirations. At the start, before I wrote a word, there was legend of *Sir Gawain and the Green Night*—a tale that's resonated with me ever since I read it as a small boy.

I often find myself pondering how the magic works in these stories—that the Green Knight survives beheading doesn't bother me so much. That he can still speak, while headless, confounds my admittedly shaky understanding of how lungs and vocal cords work. This is the kind thing I start poking with a stick, figuring it will transform into a story before too long.

Another thread of the story emerged when I researched the history of executions for another project I was working on, and finding some rather explicit descriptions of how to hang someone in terrain that's devoid of trees.

Our methods have evolved considerably over the centuries, and this led me to wonder how exactly you'd go about killing a medieval immortal using the science available to us in the twenty-first century. The magic used to withstand the trauma of a sharp sword might not be so adept at dealing with being thrown into a nuclear reactor, for example, or fired into the emptiness of space and left to asphyxiate.

Why solidified all this inspiration into a story was re-reading Peter Carey's first short story collection, *The Fat Man in History*. He's better known as a literary writer, but Carey's short fiction is shot through with speculative concepts, embracing the conceits of the slipstream genre before Bruce Sterling gave it a name. Carey has an incredible knack of contrasting the bizarre against the bureaucratic, and couples them with a sharp ear for narrative voice and a discontinuous narrative style.

The moment I jotted down the title of this story, and noted the wry irony bound into the concept, this became my attempt at writing a Peter Carey story. It quickly taught me how delicately balanced his approach can be—you're leaning fragments of a whole up against each other, leaving spaces for the reader to fill in.

ABOUT THE AUTHOR

PETER M. BALL is an author, publisher, and RPG gamer whose love of speculative fiction emerged after exposure to *The Hobbit*, *Star Wars*, David Lynch's *Dune*, and far too many games of *Dungeons and Dragons* before the age of 7. He's spent the bulk of his life working as a creative writing tutor, with brief stints as a perfor-  mance poet, gaming convention organiser, online content developer, non-profit arts manager, GenreCon convenor, and d20 RPG publisher.

He's the author of the Miriam Aster series and the Keith Murphy Urban Fantasy Thrillers, three short story collections, and more stories, articles, poems, and RPG material than he'd care to count. He's the brain-in-charge at Brain Jar Press, and resides in Brisbane, Australia, with his partner and a very affectionate cat.

Peter can be found online at:
www.petermball.com

 facebook.com/Petermball

twitter.com/petermball

 instagram.com/petermball

ALSO BY PETER M. BALL

BRAIN JAR PRESS SHORT FICTION LAB

The Early Experiments

Winged, With Sharp Teeth

8 Minutes Of Usable Daylight

A White Cross Beside A Lonely Road

One Last First Date Before The End Of The World

SHORT STORY COLLECTIONS

The Birdcage Heart & Other Strange Tales

Not Quite The End Of the World Just Yet: Short Stories & Strange Futures

These Strange & Magic Things: Short Stories

KEITH MURPHY URBAN FANTASY THRILLERS

Exile

Frost

Crusade

MIRIAM ASTER NOVELLAS

Horn

Bleed

ESSAYS

You Don't Want To Be Published & Other Things Nobody Tells You When You First Start Writing